ROSA

LEO POLITI

CHARLES SCRIBNER'S SONS

27058

ROSA lived with her mother and father and her brother José near the little village of San Felipe in Mexico. They lived in a house on the slope of a hill overlooking the desert.

Every day Rosa and José rode their horse Polomo to the village school. There were many interesting things to see on the way. There were squirrels, wild rabbits, lizards, and other small animals.

Cactus plants grew along the winding trail and birds built their nests in these plants. Sometimes Rosa and José saw tiny eggs and baby birds in the nests.

Near the village they passed little adobe houses enclosed by fences. In the yards there were pigs and goats and chickens and beautiful flowers.

Once a lazy dog was sleeping in the middle of the road and never even moved as they went by.

This was Rosa's first year at school. She was learning to read and write and draw.

At recess time the boys and girls played games. Rosa liked to play gato y raton (cat and mouse).

Everyone held hands in a circle. The cat outside the circle tried to break through and catch the mouse inside the circle. Rosa held hands with all her might. But when the cat broke through, she let the mouse out and everyone

held tight again to keep the cat inside the circle. This made the chase very exciting.

Some boys and girls played with a toy called valero. The valero is a wooden ball with a hole in it. It is attached to a stick by a string. The player throws the ball into the air and as it comes down, he tries to put the stick into the hole. This is hard to do. Whenever someone succeeded, Rosa became very excited.

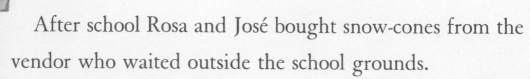

After school Rosa and José bought snow-cones from the vendor who waited outside the school grounds.

On their way home they always stopped to look in the window of the toy store. In the center of the window was a baby doll. It was a beautiful doll that came from a far-away city.

One day Rosa saw the shop owner lift up the doll. She watched with wonder as the doll's eyes opened and closed. She even heard the doll cry like a real baby.

Rosa thought that if the doll were hers it would be like having a playmate at home. She knew the doll was too expensive for her father to buy. But still she hoped that some day the doll would belong to her.

José told her that if she wished for the doll hard enough, perhaps her wish would come true.

When summer came and the nights were warm, Rosa's family slept outdoors. Rosa would fall asleep counting the stars. On each star she wished very hard for the beautiful doll in the store window.

But the summer wasn't much fun for Rosa. All during vacation José helped Father work their vegetable farm and Mother was busy cooking and cleaning.

Rosa was lonely.

Sometimes she went to the edge of the hill and looked toward San Felipe. She knew her school friends who lived in the village would be playing together.

She thought more and more of the doll in the window.

Then summer ended and school began again. The days went by quickly. Christmastime was near. Rosa wished harder than ever and hoped that her present would be the beautiful doll.

On the day before Christmas the village church bell began to ring. Its lovely sound echoed through the desert.

Dressed in their best clothes, Rosa and José went to the village. Father gave them five pesos to spend as they pleased.

The village looked festive and gay.

Large colorful pinatas hung in the public square. Pinatas are jars filled with sweets and little toys. They are covered with papier-mâché made into beautiful shapes.

Vendors sold fruits, cookies and candies, and toys at their booths.

There were tempting things everywhere.

"Feliz Navidad! Merry Christmas!" everyone greeted each other.

José wanted to buy the baby doll for Rosa, but they had only five pesos and the doll cost much more. So José bought two valeros from the toy vendor, one for Rosa and one for himself. With the money that was left, they bought cookies and gave them to Polomo.

They had lots of fun.

When Rosa and José rode home, it was almost dusk. The lights flickering inside their house looked bright and gay.

"I feel something wonderful has happened," Rosa said to José.

As they entered the house, they heard a little cry. Rosa ran into the bedroom.

There was her mother holding a newborn baby! Rosa could hardly believe her eyes.

"Que querida! What a little dear!" she cried.

"We named her Angelita. Little angel," said Mother.

"She really does look like a little angel," said José.

Everyone looked at the baby sleeping in her mother's arms. Even Polomo peered through the window to see.

Suddenly Rosa remembered her wish. José was right! Her wish had come true. She did not get the doll in the store window, but a baby sister was even better. Now she would have a real playmate.

Rosa looked at her mother and father and José, and at Angelita sleeping so peacefully.

"Feliz Navidad," Rosa whispered.

This book is also available in a Spanish edition.